HEALING BALM
HIDDEN DESIRE

HEALING BALM
HIDDEN DESIRE

ADAM KOVYNIA

Contents

Dedicated to **Anthony Robbins, Brian Tracy, and Wayne Dyer.** Your speeches and writings helped inspire me to follow my dreams and learn what's possible.

I

I had this dream last night - I wonder what Jane would think of it. It's a recurring dream, actually. I had it maybe half a dozen times over the years. The dream places me back in high school, sometimes in English class with an overwhelming amount of work to complete by the end of the week. I'll leave the interpreting to Jane. She's a psychologist, after all. I've been feeling a bit restless and frustrated since the dream, although it's also work that is getting to me.

I'm an assistant manager at a hotel, and more than anybody, I'm left to fill in the empty spaces when someone calls out. Last week it was Ron, our night auditor, who called out two nights in a row. So, I covered from 11 p.m. until 7 a.m., struggling to keep my eyes open around the middle of the shift. Today I'm in at three in the afternoon and tomorrow bright and early-that's what you call a "turnaround shift". In other words, it's the type of scheduling that leaves an associate without enough time to sleep! But anyways, Jane's place is only five minutes down the road from me, and work is fifteen minutes past her. I came to the realization lately that one reason I've reconnected with her is because she's located directly on the way to my hotel.

I slipped in my car and started the engine. A CD began playing which was a 1980s new wave compilation. I took a sip out of my water bottle and turned the corner. Jane and I had only a friendship and never anything romantic. Hard to believe it's been close to twenty years since we first became acquainted as seniors in high school. Neither of us has ever married anyone. It's in the absence of her ex-boyfriend Rick that I feel more comfortable being her friend. He's been out of the picture for at least a year now but naturally she's been in relationships with subsequent men. Yet recently she's updated her Facebook profile to indicate she's single after the most recent breakup.

I pulled into the Avalon Condominium complex where Jane resided, clearly a step up from my simple, drab apartment building, and sprayed on some cologne. Gravity is a masculine, strong, earthy scent. It comes in a dark blue, rectangular bottle. I mainly wore it for nostalgic reasons, ordering a gift set of four classic fragrances of the 90s. Walking up to her small but neat, fresh looking abode, I rang the doorbell. "Come on in Jake."

I sat down at her dining room table, sinking deeply into the extra thick cushion, resting my forearms on the table and looking over at her in the kitchen.

"You're wearing cologne. I like that scent."

I'm glad she noticed.

"Thank you. Can I have a coffee?"

"Sure."

I didn't want to leave too soon. I was only there to drop off some DVDs for her to borrow and head to work, but I still had at least twenty minutes to kill before I needed to head out.

"So, did you have any interesting dreams last night you want to tell me about?" she asked while brushing her wavy dirty-blonde hair to the side. Her thick, rectangular, black framed eyeglasses resting on her cute button nose. Pretty grey eyes were behind those glasses. She was wearing just a plain tee shirt and a pair of blue jeans.

Maybe it was a good omen or something – her asking me about my dreams. But I was going to bring it up anyways.

"Well, you know when you have recurring dreams? I had this one: I'm back in high school English class. My desk has a bunch of books on it. Too many papers. My backpack is heavy. I'm overwhelmed. You know I was an above average student or at the least average. I didn't flunk out or anything. But in the dream, I just can't seem to get on track..." I went on.

"Here's your coffee." She walked over to the table and placed the mug next to me.

"Jake, you know that, generally, people who dream about not being prepared for an exam in school are the same people who are *overprepared* in real life and typically get straight A's!" Jane responded.

"Hmm interesting."

"You were a studious guy in high school I remember. At least you played the part well. Mr.

preppy, Five Star. You've got that Clark Kent thing going on."

It's probably the third time in my life I've been compared to Clark Kent, which I take as a compliment although I'm average height rather than being tall and I'm thick and stocky these days although trying to lose weight, I thought to myself.

"Five Star? Oh, like the notebook? I'd like to try to forget most of those days."

"Think of it as a positive," Jane said.

"Okay, so I was a bit of a square? I can accept that, at this point. How many years have gone by since then, right?"

"The past is the past, and by the way, if you don't remember, I was way more of a geek than you. Right?"

She might have been, but I won't tell her that. It kind of bothers me that I never made a move on her, romantically, all these years. But that whole bookworm, intellectual thing is very sexy to me now. Not so much then, I suppose.

Looking at her, I suddenly see her in a sexual way.

"How's the coffee?" she asked while making eye contact with me from across the room. It felt as if we were right next to each other. Funny how non-verbal communication, such as eye contact, can tell a story. Like the two of us knowing there's a connection in that look we just gave each other. I'm usually not the type to make eye contact with people for more than an instant. I'm just more introverted in that sense.

"Well doctor, what can you tell me about *your* dreams last night?"

"Hmmm, well, let me see if I can remember them...I'll have to get back to you on that."

I took another sip of coffee and savored it, zoning out, looking at a series of trees out the window. I was stretching my time out like a piece of putty, not caring if I would be late to work. It was unlike me because I was always conscientious of my responsibilities. Was I finally ready to let go of the same old dull routine?

"Tell me something interesting about body language," I said.

She had a playful smile and her eyes turned up to the corner of the ceiling. "Body language huh?"

"Yeah." I made sure to look over at her again, intently, and into her eyes, albeit still from a distance, as she was back in the kitchen resting her arm against the wall. I then looked down at her bare feet. Her toenails, painted indigo. Slowly, my eyes made their way up, checking her out in those tight jeans that hugged her soft body. Her thick thighs and slightly wide hips drove me crazy. I can see she became red by blushing and ran her right hand through her long strands of hair.

Walking towards me, she placed her hand gently on my forearm, exciting me immediately and leaving me anticipating what would happen next. "When a woman makes physical contact with a guy like this during conversation, it could be a sign that she finds him attractive and acceptable. In other words, she's interested."

"Oh, well, yes, that is good to know."

"I like that cologne...mmm."

"Here, smell it under the wrist where I sprayed some." I raised my arm towards her face, and she held my forearm while sniffing the fragrance. Just her hand holding my forearm was magic. After a second, she sniffed again, and this time pressed her nose and lips to my wrist while taking in the scent.

A silence, lasting a few seconds, came between us, but our silences were never awkward in a bad way. Maybe only awkward because of the sexual tension between us, which actually felt good.

"Well, I have those DVD's I came to drop off for you," I said.

"Oh yeah, the Forensic Files. Sometime after I start watching them, we'll discuss."

"I don't know what it is, but true crime, I love to watch. Like we've watched together. You know, the Dateline NBC stuff, ABC 20/20...all that but the *fictional* crime...I have trouble getting into it."

"I'm the same way, we have that in common." She looked over at the clock. "Aren't you going to be late?" she said with some urgency.

"Yeah I better get going. I'm so sick of this hotel. Last week, two graveyard shifts. Today I'm on till 11 p.m. and then tomorrow I'm on for 7 a.m. Bright and early. You know what that means?" I asked.

"What Jake?"

"It means by the time I get home and unwind...I'll only have a couple hours to sleep, then I'll be up watching the early morning news with a strong cup of coffee and a cool shower to jolt the senses."

Jane looked at me, in a loving, tender way. Was

it the psychologist in her? I mean, *come on*. All these years and never *anything* between us. She couldn't really like me the way I wanted her to all of a sudden, could she? It's not like she'd ever called me *cute* or anything like that. Well, she did compliment the way I was dressed, a couple of times, stating I looked good. That could count for something. And we did spend all this time together over the years. On and off at that, *but still.*

We stood next to each other. I wanted time to stand still because I much preferred being in her condo as opposed to going to work. "Bye," she said, stretching out the word.

I swung the door behind me and walked to my car.

2

So, I arrived to work ten minutes late, but nobody said a word. I did apologize to Steve and told him I'd come in an extra fifteen minutes early to relieve him next time. Would Jane say that it's my attempt to be Mr. nice guy by always helping and even sometimes being a pushover? I eased into the day and made myself a cup of cheap coffee from our free coffee station. Soft rock music played in the background at a comfortable volume. A song by the band The Fray. I tapped my fingers on the counter, matching the rhythm. Taking a couple of deep breaths calmed me down. I made some key packets in advance and stocked up my front desk area with copy paper, rubber bands, pens, staples, notepads, etc.

"Beth, do you mind watering those plants there? You see we have four of them...." I pointed out where they were placed in our lobby. Our general manager, Raul, picked them up from the nursery last week. Beth was new, and I was showing her the ropes around here, so I couldn't leave her behind the desk all on her own.

While she took off to tend to the plant life, I took a sip of my nasty coffee and chewed on grinds which were mixed into the hot beverage. At least it was not lukewarm. Well, there's something about a cheap coffee while on the job that's better than a cheap coffee off the clock in a way. When you're at work, it's a treat you deserve. A reward for your hard work, I suppose - a way to take your mind off your humdrum tasks. I daydreamed about Jane. Miss Jane PHD. What the hell was I thinking all this time...all these years. She was sexy as ever in a sort of girl next door, plain-Jane type of way. No pun intended. That whole plain-Jane thing is not a negative. Her plainness made her lovely and alluring. Was she really plain after all? If beauty is in the eye of the beholder, then what is plainness? It's all relative, I guess. All that mattered to me now was having a chance with her. Would I have the

courage after all these years of on and off friendship to take things to the next level? Would she accept or reject me? It's now or never. Neither one of
us is getting any younger. Nor are we guaranteed
another day in life.

I drove home late that night, passing by her
condo as I always do since it's directly on the way. I
cracked open the windows in my car to let in cool
air. I saw the stars and a waxing crescent moon in
the peaceful sky. No, I wasn't going to stop in, but
I kept thinking about her. We're both single now.
How long will this potential opportunity last? I
got home and prepared a bath for myself. Lighting two large unscented candles and pouring two
capfuls of my favorite green aromatic bubble bath.
It's a rare and mysterious scent, no longer being
produced. Luckily, people still sell twenty-year old
bottles of the stuff online, with the seals still in-
tact. I turned the dial, releasing a stream of hot
water crashing into the thick green liquid, creat-
ing bubbles and steam while the candle gave off
enough light to make the room feel cozy. I laid
in the tub resting my back flush against the bottom and feeling the heat of the water circulate the
flow of blood throughout my body. That was it. In

that moment, the scales finally tipped in the direction of me deciding I'd make a move with Jane. What did I have to lose? I'd likely lose my friendship with her when she'd find another man soon enough, or worse yet, she'd get married, have a kid. Several kids. A dog. A cat. Next thing you know I'd be lucky to get a Christmas card and just remain friends with her on Facebook.

I wonder what she thinks of my body. I know I must lose weight, but I'm not terribly heavy or anything like that. But burning off that excess fat would allow my muscles to pop and for sure people would notice that. I suppose it depends on who you ask. It's all relative, I thought.

The bath relaxed my mind and muscles so well that when I hit the bed, I fell right asleep. However, it was past midnight and I got up at 3:45 a.m. I could not fall back asleep. I lay in bed thinking of who else but Jane. I'd never thought of her so much all these years and quite like this. I imagined her wearing those black spandex pants she does sometimes. Her butt being squeezed by the tight fabric. Her soft and fluffy medium-sized breasts bulging outward like balloons. I fantasized about her while in bed. Later tossing and turning and finally giving up on attempting sleep. I jumped out of bed and made myself a coffee and a bowl of raisin bran cereal with a handful of walnuts tossed in, then took a refreshing shower. Got dressed in a white shirt and black tie, black pants and a sports coat.

When I got to work, I had an electric energy about me. The lack of sleep would likely catch up to me at some point. Raul, the hotel's General Manager, walked in the main entrance and threw up a hand which held a bag of food. "Jake!" He held three coffees in one of those four cup cardboard carrier trays in his other hand.

I'd put in at least half an hour by then, and Raul asked Beth to cover the desk while he treated me to a coffee and muffin outside. It's sink or swim for Beth, but sooner or later she'd have to be on her own behind the desk. The weather is pleasant at 63 degrees in early May. Exiting the building, we took a seat on the bench by the weeping cherry tree around the corner.

Raul is a friend. We got along great. He's the top guy at our hotel; I'm second in command. And as much as I've had it with my job lately, it's people like him that make work tolerable, even fun sometimes through laughs and conversation.

"Thanks for the coffee."

"By the way, this is a protein muffin with mixed fruit and pumpkin seeds. Don't worry, I got one for Beth also," Raul said.

"Raul, that's it! I'm going to make another date with Jane again today after I get out of here." I took a big bite out of my muffin. Took a sip of coffee, still hot and so good compared to what we had in the hotel's free coffee station. "This is good. What is this, like a dark roast?"

"French Roast, and by the way, sixteen grams of protein in the muffin. Jane huh, that's your Doctor friend there, right?"

"Oh yeah and I shouldn't have said *date* because I never had an actual date with her. We're friends," I said.

"She is smart. Obviously," Raul responded with his characteristic accent, "she is hmm how do I say, not the most beautiful woman but it's her stability that you're attracted to, I think."

"I don't know. I sure like stability, who doesn't? I think she's really sexy and I just can't get her out of my mind Raul. I couldn't even get back to sleep this morning. I just think about wanting to reach towards her and kiss her and ..."

"And...what else. You know I'm a gay man, but I'm still interested in hearing all this," Raul responded.

"I want to take off those tight black pants and pull down her panties slowly and.."

"Wow, I never heard you talk like this Jake," Raul smiled while reaching for his coffee, then taking a bite out of his muffin.

"It's because I'm actually saying how I feel. You know?"

"I know you're human. We all are."

I glanced down at my watch. "After I get out of here at three, I'll stop by her place. It's on the way and I'll call her first to see if she wants to watch a show on TV or something."

"What about Beth, do you like her?"

"Beth, she's okay, sure. But she's a coworker, I'm a manager."

"I know... I'm just seeing how horny you really are!" Raul said, laughing.

"Are you kidding me? I think about women more than you realize!"

"You can't just stop at her place like this, right? Dressed in your shirt and tie? And you need to bring a bottle of wine...some food?"

"OK yeah so that's not a bad suggestion. I'll do that."

3

I stopped in at Jane's. I loved her place. The fresh paint, bold colors in different rooms, the soft carpet you just sink into. The comfortable couch. She had these South American and African masks hanging on the walls. And she had this collection of colorful glasses, vases, paintings on the wall she'd bought at a local gallery.

"I thought we'd watch a true crime show, since we both like that," I mentioned.

"Sure."

"Thank you for bringing that bottle of wine," she said while pouring each of us a glass and leaving the rest of the bottle on the dining room table. She took a sip. It was a thick, sweet, and strong apricot wine. "Oh, that's so good."

She came back in the living room with a container of Chinese food in her hand. "It's vegetable lo mein, and I have a fresh block of tofu on the kitchen counter if you'd like to help me prepare it - we can add it to the dish."

Jane was a vegetarian since before I can remember, which kind of intrigued me. I'd even thought about it today and how I'd deliberately try to avoid eating meat around her. Maybe that would even make an impression on her, for all I know.

"Come on into the kitchen for a minute." She paused the program we were watching on TV.

Jane turned the dial on a kitchen gadget and out fell a block of tofu landing on a layer of paper towels.

"A tofu-press?" I asked.

"Exactly! You *know* what it's called! I'm impressed. I couldn't even find one of these in any of the kitchen stores I went to including the gourmet shops. So, what did I do? Well of course I bought it online," Jane said with a grin.

She was wearing loose-fitting, white, full leg linen pants and a blouse. Again, barefoot with those beautifully painted toenails. She couldn't fail to attract me whether it was loose pants, tight pants or whatever....I think I'm in love.

I walked over closer towards her to see what she was doing. Pressing the paper towels over the tofu and squeezing the remaining moisture out is what she was doing. I thought to myself: I'd like to taste her tofu.

"You know... I don't bite. You can come closer," she said.

It's weird. I've heard people say that to me more than once in my life. I think I need her to counsel me through it. She's a psychologist after all. Jane took a big kitchen knife and sliced through the tofu, making cubes about one inch in size. I just opened my mouth and leaned forward so she got the clue and picked up a fork. Stabbing a cube of tofu, she lifted it in the air and placed it in my mouth. I chewed the cool, smooth, white substance made from soybeans.

"OK Jake, no more raw tofu for us. Let's fry it up. Can you hand me the vegetable oil? It's underneath, to your left."

We started working on it and I stood back to observe her from the side. I could see the outline of her underwear beneath the thin layer of clothing she was wearing. It drove me wild. I don't know what's gotten into me lately.

Then we sat and watched the program, sipping wine, enjoying our vegetable lo mein and fried tofu. Two little bottles of sauce sat on the coffee table. One red, the hot sauce, and one dark brown, the hoisin. Pouring some of each over our food every now and then made it sweet and fragrant plus gave it a kick.

"So, this guy is a pastor of sorts... I saw this one already. Full disclosure," I said.

"OK, but don't tell me what happens next," Jane pleaded.

"No, I won't," I enjoyed chewing on the food and the textures of the noodles and crunchy carrots, zucchini, baby corn and tofu. There was a bit of saltiness and a bit of sweetness to it. A bit of garlic flavor maybe also. Definitely comfort food, I'd say. It didn't even need that extra sauce we poured over it but that made it so delectable. "This is good. I can eat this stuff every day," I said.

She turned her head towards me and smiled. Jane had milky white skin and those tiny freckles dotting her checks and nose were so cute.

"So, they make a hot couple," Jane said, referring to the show we were watching.

"Yeah, I like this one, definitely one of my favorite episodes."

We talked throughout the show, discussing our personal opinions on the case. I realized how much she and I had in common. For instance, we both had a similar taste in music over the years and we both had a stylish conservative look when it came to clothes. I'd never really found someone who liked to watch these shows with me, and I think that's essential for a relationship-*to like the same things.*

"I found myself worked up about the whole case when I first watched it a few months back, ready to type a comment on YouTube about how this guy sure is some kind of pastor, you know, big hypocrite. Doing hard drugs, partying, having sex without being married. You know, all that stuff, but then I start to read people's comments and it's as if they took the words out of my mouth. Comment after comment bashing the guy, so then I thought: what's the point in writing the comment I was about to write? It's kind of obvious, you know? Yeah, he was a bit of a hypocrite leading sort of a double life and sinning but then again as long as he's not guilty of the murder in this case, what did he really do so wrong?"

"I would have to agree with you Jake. Taking drugs-personal choice. The Sex? It's not like he was going around with more than one woman. It was only him and her, as far as we can tell, plus he was ready to propose to her. That was his plan, so he said anyways. I think he had a need somewhere deep down that was unfulfilled," Jane said.

"It's weird, you know, sometimes, society sees things in such a black and white way. I think a lot of overly religious people have just as much of a dark side to them as the next guy though. Maybe we need to learn to be less judgmental of others and more accepting," I responded.

"It sure would create a lot less tension within us if we just let go of judging everyone...do you hear that? Someone's at the door," she said.

Then a few more knocks came, and Jane got up to peer through the window blinds. "It's Rick."

I really didn't like Rick. OK, I hated him. "You're dating him now?" I asked.

"No...I haven't seen him in ages. I'm going to get the door; what do you want to do?"

"I'm getting out the back door. We finished the show and it's probably time I head out," I responded.

In a hurry, I got out of there, not wanting Rick to get the wrong idea. I'd never been romantic with Jane before and why give him the wrong idea. He's aggressive. He's also a big guy at six foot two and according to just about every woman who's met him, a gorgeous hunk. I've heard all the descriptions: tall, dark, and handsome, hot and on and on. Personally, with him back on the scene, I don't feel I'm ever going to find out what my romantic life would be like with Jane at this point.

4

When I got home, I signed in online using my laptop. I grabbed an ice-cold, amber lager European style beer from the fridge. Just my luck, I bet Jane and Rick will share the remainder of wine I bought! I got to get it off my mind.

Raul sent me a message online. I quickly typed back and let him know the general summary of how my evening went. "Let me see a picture of this guy Rick?" Raul asked.

I lead him to where he could see the pictures of Rick on Facebook and I didn't care for Raul's response. "You're going to have to compete with that guy?!" he typed. "Maybe find another woman Jake."

"Listen Raul, I'm not going to *compete* with any

guy for Jane. It's either she wants me, or she doesn't," I wrote.

"Maybe she wants a man to step up and make the first move? Did you ever think of that Mr. Jakey?"

"*Of course*, but look, if you go to Jane's page, you can see she still has at least some old photos of her and Rick."

"Hmm, you know, I think she wants him and can't let him go, because not only is he gorgeous, but I think he's like a trophy boyfriend for her. She's a psychologist. She can support him. No, maybe it's not that. Maybe it's that she feels like she's special because *he* wants her. I don't know, it's like they're an unlikely couple or something," Raul wrote.

"I give up on her. Too much trouble Raul. I'm having some beer and I'm heading to bed."

5

I found myself peacefully drifting away in bed. The mattress absorbed my achy body, and soon, I was sound asleep. In my dream I was driving. I had a Zen like state of mind. The music was just right; a fresh coffee rested in the cup holder. The temperature was pleasant, and the air was fresh in the car. It felt calm and effortless while I took each curve along a smooth road and observed a natural landscape around me. I discovered a plaza which I stopped at. I saw many businesses there, and I always like to explore each and everything in a place that makes me feel good. This place gave me that vibe.

I saw a fitness center, and inside, a woman with bright blonde hair pulled back. She was sweating and straining on a stair stepper. She looked Scandinavian. If I had to guess, 100 percent Swedish. Everyone was busy exercising along that window looking out at the cars. I could see a neon sign inside the gym which read *Sauna*. In the same plaza, a health food store and a chocolate shop. A florist. A comic book shop. Everything was brand new to me here. No recognition of these places at all for me.

I drove around the perimeter at about ten or fifteen miles per hour then turned right into another plaza which revealed a lake in the distance. There was a pizzeria. Immediately I felt excited about that, my mouth almost watering. I figured I'd get myself a small pie later to take home, and I'd stop at the liquor store next door to pick up some rum and a case of beer. Suddenly I was transported inside the nearby coffee house. There was this mixed scent in the air of roasting and brewing coffee, but it was stronger than what I was used to. What I imagine heaven to be like anyways. Or what I've read about in those near-death experience books where your senses are heightened. While I sat there and sipped from my mug, I talked with a friend named Luke. Luke was like someone

I'd felt I'd known in real life, but really it was just an illusion, because I knew nobody of the such in my waking life. Our friendship seemed very real, and there was an equality between us. Like we were best buds. The guys and gals playing pool in the distance were also friends of mine in the dream. I felt so at ease and free to be in this place. Everything about it just felt safe and serene. It's like a weight was lifted off me.

"Misty came around asking about you again Jake," Luke said with a smile.

"Where is she? When can I meet her?" I asked, feeling a sense of urgency.

Kenny walked over towards us, resting his pool stick against the wall.

"Right Kenny?" Luke asked.

"We can fix you up with Misty if you want. You guys will make a great couple."

When I woke up, I started feverishly writing down every detail of the dream. The smells in the air-pine trees, cedar, the lake, the fogginess in the atmosphere at certain points in the dream. The smacking sound of the pool balls being broken up. I remember seeing someone drinking a blue slushy drink in a clear cup with a straw. I imagined what it would taste like. Even the flavor of the coffee left an impression on me. Like I could still taste it on my tongue while I sat up awake in bed.

That was it I decided. If I'm not going to pursue Jane, then I would find Misty, but in real life. No, she doesn't have to be named Misty, but if she were, then sure, that would be an amazing premonition. Nevertheless, as crazy as it sounded, the dream was more than just an ordinary dream, considering how I felt during it. This was God sending me a message. And Jane's ex-boyfriend Rick, well... him showing up at Jane's condo must have meant something too. I'm a big believer in the concept of 'everything happens for a reason' in our waking life, and in our dream life, I believe everything has a meaning for us to learn from and use to improve our waking life, maybe improve the lives of others in the process.

6

Work was becoming more and more monotonous, yet I took it in stride. I managed to block all reservations into the appropriate rooms requested except for one. The man reserved a suite with two beds, and we only have a few in our entire building, so unfortunately due to one family extending their stay, it created a shortage of that specific room type. The good news was that I'd be likely gone before they show up to check in since I'd only work until 3 p.m., and the bulk of our check ins arrive later than that, for sure. Of course, the evening or overnight workers likely will be stuck with the unenviable task. I guess the thing I hate the most about this business is that when the hypothetical family does check in and the guy or gal behind the counter has to give them the bad news that we don't have their particular request, the family checking in will likely take out their frustration on the associate. It's hard particularly if you're sensitive, and let's face it—it's not the associate's fault most of the time. Behind the scenes, the top executives have a system to allow for greater revenue by overbooking on purpose. The real sad reality of human nature is that if sometimes the boss is at fault for something, the customer feels more intimidated by the boss, aka the authority figure, and will generally only take out their frustrations on the lower rung associate.

The bright side of my current life situation was that my dream of the lake, the plaza, mysterious town and all plus Misty were strong in my mind. I could feel it in my bones. Something was so meaningful about it; I couldn't just let it disappear from my conscious mind. Even the feeling of relief I felt in the dream. It goes to show I'm carrying around too much tension in my day to day waking life. First thing I need to start with is losing weight again. I had the calculator up on the screen and realized that at my current weight I'd have to lose forty pounds in order to really get to where I wanted to-lean and mean- but even ten pounds lost would make a visible difference.

And then the phone rang. I responded with my cheerful greeting, and surprisingly I heard from Jane on the other end.

"Hi Jane. You've never called the hotel line before. Must be important."

"If you're busy, I can call you later. I just figured if you're free, I'd like to clear something up."

"Sure."

"OK... so, I didn't hear from you and to be fair, I hadn't gotten back to you either yet but I just want you to know that Rick is leaving town to do a construction project. Actually, he's leaving the state. Georgia. That's a far distance Jake. He wanted to stop by because he just said he found himself thinking about me and he was in town visiting some friends and all," Jane explained.

"OK."

"Are you mad Jake? Taking off that night so abruptly when Rick showed up and all."

"No, I'm glad you called."

"OK, well, take care Jake."

Raul walked by. "Are you OK Jake? You look lost in space."

"Yeah, I'll be fine."

"Come on, tell me what's going on."

"Well, Rick is out of state and out of the picture, I suppose."

"Great. Now's your chance! Go for it with Doctor Jane."

"Maybe you're right, but honestly, I'm intimidated by the guy. Plus, I still don't know her true feelings for me. She probably just thinks of me as a friend."

"Jake, I just had a burst of insight."

"I'm listening..." I said.

"Would you consider buying counseling sessions from Jane?"

"Oh, that's weird," I responded.

"No wait, you remember how you ask her questions about psychology and have her interpret your dreams."

"Hmmm actually I think you're on to something." I stopped to ponder the situation for a moment. "When or if Rick comes back to town and develops a relationship with Jane again after his construction project, it would be safe to be around her because I'd be her client receiving counseling. Strictly Business. She could even tell him that, and what could he do about it? Otherwise, if I don't ask her to do this for me, I'd be nudged out of the way by Rick. I've seen this guy get jealous and physical with other people who'd flirted with her. I don't need that kind of drama in my life," I said.

"Call her right away Jake. There's no shame in that. Do it now, seize the day!"

I picked up the phone and dialed Jane.

"Hi Jake," she said.

"Listen Jane, I'm going to just jump right in and ask you something. You're great at what you do. I wanted to tell you that. How would you feel about taking me on for a therapy session? I know..I know it sounds like an odd thing for me to ask you probably."

"Actually, I'd be honored. When are you available to start?"

That's another thing I loved about Jane. She was ready and eager to go. Those are the kind of people that we need in the world.

"How about this evening?"

"Come on by at say, seven, after you eat dinner."

7

⸙

I ate a light dinner at home. It was spinach cooked in olive oil along with fresh cubes of potatoes with chickpeas sautéed also in oil with turmeric, cumin, ground pepper, and salt. An Indian dish. Eagerly awaiting my session with her, I had a nervous butterfly thing going on in my stomach but in a good way. I arrived at her place at a quarter to seven in the evening. Jane came to the door out of breath, still wearing her exercise clothing, sweat rolling down her cheeks. Droplets of sweat on her chest. Her cleavage revealed by a sports bra. Spandex pants and colorful sneakers as well. "You're early. That's OK if you don't mind waiting for me to take a shower."

I sat on the cozy couch once more and flipped

through channels on the television for a couple minutes but felt restless. I had the urge to get some fresh air and stretch my legs. Women take forever to get ready after all. I got up from the couch and walked towards the door. I considered leaving a note but realized I shouldn't leave the door unlocked, so I walked down the hallway glancing into her bedroom and saw her standing with a bath towel in her hand, still sweaty but getting ready to take her shower.

"Do you mind if I take a walk around the neighborhood while you get ready?"

"Sure. Just take my keys with you and lock up. I'll be super quick. I promise."

As I walked outside and felt the pleasant breeze upon my face, I decided to take a left and walk along the curved road, enjoying the charming condos along the way. A squirrel crossed the path in front of me. I came to a bulletin board with what had to be a hundred things posted to it. You know the kind where one person is tacking their business card on top of another person's and they've run out of push pins. I saw everything there being advertised, from wildlife artists, wedding photographers, plumbing, even the construction company Rick worked for. It was likely Jane had one somewhere here advertising her psychotherapy sessions. I couldn't miss the biggest advertisement in the upper right-hand corner since it was the size of a mini poster. An Asian woman who went by the name Miyuki singing at a piano. *Blue Spruce Jazz club*, it was for this Friday evening. I can make that. Maybe it's a sign. After that dream I'd had with the mysterious Misty by the lake and all. I like smooth jazz music after all, and this could be my chance to meet someone new.

As I made my way back to Jane's place, I waited another couple of minutes and she was ready, hair tied up in a bun, wearing a pair of khakis and a business-like pleated top. OK so she looked beautiful, but in my mind, she was back to being a friend only. The same way she'd been all these years I'd known her. Ever since we were seniors in high school, I'd figured deep down that I wasn't good enough for her because she was a straight A student. Maybe I was just damaged after years of never quite fitting in most of the time. And then, as I evolved along the way, there were always other reasons why her and I never made it past the friendship zone, Rick being one of those reasons. Simply put, I was here to get a counseling session.

"Let's begin by taking a deep breath. Slowly in through the nose and hold it there. Gently exhale through the mouth. Forget about conventional therapy. We can always do the traditional thing another time down the road. OK now I want you to tell me about a dream you've had," Jane said.

"There was a dream that I had where I was a kid on the playground at around seven, maybe eight years old. It was in the Wintertime, so I had my heavy jacket on and a winter hat. Someone...I don't know who, took off my hat and threw it to another kid. So, I went to try to grab it and I could never get a hold of it, as hard as I tried. The thing is that even the girls who were the most well behaved in the class were keeping my hat away from me. I was surprised they would do that. All they had to do was just hand it to me," I explained.

"Jake, I want you to be really honest with me. Did something like this really happen to you in life or was it only a dream?" she asked.

"It actually happened," I responded.

"What lesson do you walk away with from this all? Remember, you've had a lot of years pass by since this happened," Jane said while jotting notes on her clipboard.

"Hmm, well, even though all the kids involved on the playground that day were wrong by what they did, nobody's perfect. We all make mistakes in life. I think that if people are thinking clearly though, they're going to do the right thing if it's simple enough. But too often, people are not thinking clearly. They're all reacting in a fearful way. You know the concept about people's actions coming from either a place of fear or love, nothing else. What benefit does someone get by teasing another person? It's kind of sick when you think of it. I suppose it's like putting someone down. Making fun of them etc. What's the motive behind that? Or how about something worse, like throwing objects at someone. Erasers, rocks, stuff like that. It's obviously a form of anger. It's violence."

"How about inclusion? Like at school for instance. How well did you fit in?" she asked.

"Sometimes I just plain did not fit in, but other times I did OK."

"Go on..."

"If you have something to offer another person. We're talking about back when we were kids here.

Right? So, let's say a friend in school wants to spend time with you and be your friend for a reason. There's got to be a reason why he chooses to be your friend and then later he's no longer your friend a couple years down the road. You lose touch...and if your parents aren't there to get involved and help you out, it's that much harder," I said.

"Hmm...Interesting," Jane said.

"You know it's interesting."

"What is?" She asked.

"I was just thinking about what I said about kids throwing things at other kids. Getting beat up even. I had these friends in my neighborhood and one of them was with me one day. We were talking about another kid in the neighborhood and my friend was telling me kids throw things at him in the hallway. Essentially, he was saying the kid had hardly any friends and that sort of thing. I wasn't about to tell him that I had the same problems at school myself. Here's an insight I have about that sort of thing today: why not take the kid's side who's getting bullied? If what the kids are doing is wrong, call it a sin or whatever you want. Isn't the way of Jesus to help the downtrodden? I don't mean to get super religious here, but millions of people can celebrate Christmas and Easter but what about trying to live like Jesus. Or, if you don't like Jesus, what about taking the Buddha's example?"

"Or if not Buddha, there's Sai Baba of Shirdi?' Jane said, playfully.

"You know Sai Baba said, 'If someone insults you, do not return tit for tat,' I responded.

"Sai Baba said that? You know your stuff Jake; I'm impressed," Jane responded. "It's like those kids who took your hat away. They didn't take your side. They all went along with the gang. It was the easy way out."

"I've dealt with bullying like that in different ways throughout my life, you can say, on and off over the years. I know that when I feel good about myself, things are going to be OK. At least that's the mental attitude I get-the world feels safer. It's not that I consciously think the world is unsafe when I'm feeling unhappy, but there's that sense of fear when going out there and trying new things. Say, going for a job interview or even making conversation with people. I guess I'm making a revelation today. I should do things that make me feel good about myself. Positive energy. But it's not just enough to do that. I've got to follow through and make something bigger happen like losing every last pound for instance."

"How do you like your work at the hotel? Do I really have to even ask that, after what you've told me over the years?"

"I hate it."

"You don't belong there Jake."

"I sometimes wonder if it's me or if it's the job. I know intuitively it doesn't feel right, plus the interaction between guest and associate is almost always fake. All that matters is what our scores are on the survey and how much money the company makes every day. It's like a fake world. I guess it's just the world we live in. Business. Then I think that's where I come in and question myself. Maybe I'm too sensitive. Maybe I'm lacking confidence. Then again, I feel like we're all intended to do something in life that makes us feel happy. Something we can do with joy...you're either working to make someone's goals and visions come true or you're working for yourself and making your own dreams come true," I said.

Jane repositioned herself on the couch and

tucked one leg under the other, making herself comfortable. She took a sip of water.

"Can I ask you something personal? How did you feel when you were dating Sandra?"

Sandra was a young woman, in her early twenties, who worked with me at the hotel years ago and Jane had met her because at that time we were all double dating.

"She didn't have the moral standards I was looking for really. I say that because she was dating other guys while she was dating me. Call me old fashioned but I believe in honesty and sticking to one person. I wasn't in management back then, so there was no conflict with us dating. She and I just didn't really hit it off. I think I saw it as an opportunity to try dating again. I was in such a dry spell because I felt self-conscious enough to essentially stop dating for...let me think...seven years. Even I can't believe that, but it's true," I said.

"That must have been hard."

"Well, during that time, I tried to approach dating again. I asked someone out and she said yes, but I never saw her around again. Needless to say, we never traded contact info because I figured I'd see her in class again, but she must have dropped out of college. Then there was someone who had offered to take me to church for some kind of nighttime Christian service, and we did exchange online contact info so we could chat on AOL. I marked my calendar and looked forward to that night for a couple weeks. She offered to drive and pick me up, so when the night finally came, I stood outside under the streetlight next to my on-campus apartment in the sprinkling rain for half an hour, I finally gave up and came back inside. In other words, she stood me up. It's the weirdest thing when I look back on it. Take this example that happened in the same year: I was hanging out with this classmate and she was sending me signals that she wanted to be intimate, but it wasn't all that direct either. I never made the first move with her because I really had my eyes on another class-mate. I regret that now. But when I asked out the classmate which I had the desire for, she gave me an uncertain answer that I took as a no. Turns out she had a boyfriend, but she never told me that di-rectly. No wonder she never really gave me a clear no, but I put the pieces of the puzzle together," I explained to Jane.

"Some might say what you're retelling here is an

example of *the law of attraction*. Let's say the energy and all you put out to the universe is what you're getting back. Maybe you were putting out mixed signals in what you wanted and what you felt comfortable with. Some might see it differently even. Say God or whatever word you want to use to describe this God force, if you will. Creator, divine energy, let's say, has different plans for you," Jane went on.

"Like a plan. God is in control."

"Yes. There's also the concept of being a *co-worker with God...karma... Cause and effect*. I get excited about all this stuff. How about this? You just told me about how you turned one woman's advances down and another woman turned your advances down. Things have a way of evening out. I'm thinking of that Seinfeld episode, you remember that one? But seriously, you might have seen someone in your class, let's say who you really would have loved to be with but somewhere deep inside of you-you didn't feel you deserved her," Jane explained.

"Missed opportunities, I've had a lot of those," I said. Because I was so deep into our session, there was no longer a sexual tension between her and

I but rather a cooperation between two people. Therapy. With Rick back in the picture, I didn't consider Jane an option in that way anymore either. Sure, Rick was off doing a construction project, but he'd be back soon enough.

"Jake, I want you to try something. I want you to speak to someone who you ordinarily wouldn't approach because of shyness. It's an experiment. The purpose of an experiment is to study the result and learn something. It doesn't have to guarantee a good result, but it can teach you something."

When our session ended, I reached into my pocket, taking out my wallet.

"There's no need to pay me Jake. I don't want to accept money from you for this. It's my pleasure really. But I want us to continue. Are you available, say...same time, same day next week?" she asked.

"That would be great."

"Oh, and by the way. Don't worry about the cost of next week's session either. This is something I *want* to do."

After I left her condo, I walked to my car and drove the short ride home thinking about everything I told her and how intimate my details were. I opened up to her and became so personal and vulnerable. But at this point in my life things need to change. I also gave thought to what she said about reaching out and talking to someone. An *experiment*.

8

Friday was winding down and while I was at work, I looked forward to the jazz concert this evening. When I got home from work, I did a half hour circuit training routine with my free weights on an empty stomach. Then some abdominal exercises. I took a shower and got dressed in a pair of dark blue jeans, a checkered button-down shirt that had a couple shades of blue to it with some thin lines of red and then splashed on some Cool Water cologne. I wore my glasses, as I usually do, rather than my contacts.

I still could not get that dream out of my mind. Maybe my session with Miss Jane has a connection to my dream in some way. In the dream, I had that sense of peace where a weight was lifted off me. In other words, no tension. Maybe with more therapy sessions I'd get closer to that feeling. Maybe this night out was somehow connected to my dream. Did I really need therapy anyways? It's not like I'm a really troubled guy or anything like that. But why was Jane doing the therapy for free? One thing's for sure; it's a way of keeping me anchored to Jane's world while Rick is back on her radar.

I set my GPS to the address of the jazz club. It directed me to take a left where the road forked and interestingly it was a road I'd never been down in my life. Essentially farmland to my left and woods on the other side. I traveled down it for several minutes with some slight curves and then came a lake to my right. Or was it a pond. Either way, I like it. I took in a deep breath and experienced a bit of wonder. A contemporary house with that beach house beige color and some cool geometric windows was in the distance. I love that stuff. Nature is one thing, but man-made and nature together impresses me more. I just love architecture. It has an effect on me.

Out in Forest Loop there really is not a whole lot, so I'm told anyways. Plus, it's a good 45-minute drive from where I live, and I never had the need to come out there. Here was my need. My desire. On this Friday night. OK so here I was. I parked my car and it was jamming. Hardly a spot. The building was all white stucco and had a cool looking roof. Overall, kind of an 80s look, especially with all the neon signs.

When I walked in, I felt at ease. I also had a surge of excitement like a pulse running through me. I ordered a *Blue Spruce Martini* which contained a top shelf gin, spruce flavor, and blue curacao with a lemon twist. Holding the martini glass was icy cold to the skin. I carefully sipped it so that none would spill, since it was filled to the brim. I left a tip on the counter and found a seat, blending in with the crowd. It was a fusion jazz type of music playing, which I'm not particularly a fan of. *But* it was just the opening act. I need something a little more organized than this sound, but I could enjoy it with the help of my beverage.

I did feel different here but in a stimulated, excitable, turned on, kind of way. Glancing around the room, I could see a pattern of little square windows, equally spaced apart and with black and white framed photos in between. It was all very symmetrical. Relaxed lighting. This place looked like one big square. I noticed the roof was a pyramid hip style. It's where all four sides are triangles and meet at the top. I'm here on my own. Yeah, I've become a bit of a loner, I guess. Maybe I've always been that way from the start. Miyuki took the stage. And her band was killing it. I loved the music. There was a piano, horn, sax, keyboards, drums, bass, electric guitar, even background vocals from two women wearing black dresses with dark stockings, moving their hips to the rhythm.

I repeated a trip to the bar but only this time ordering a lager beer in a pint glass. As the night wore on, I didn't regret coming here at all plus it reinforced a study I heard about on how attending concerts makes people happier and more inspired. I felt that way after seeing a Bobby Caldwell and Richard Elliott show a few years ago. I found myself singing "Heart of Mine" the next morning along with my cup of coffee in hand.

As Miyuki's show ended, I suddenly remembered how Jane wanted me to reach out and talk to someone as an experiment. I got up out of my chair and started walking in the direction of the stage. Suddenly there was Miyuki stepping through the crowd and as I came closer to her, I said, "You were excellent! Your whole band is very talented!"

"Well, thank you," she responded with a smile.

"Do you have a CD I can buy?"

"Yes. Hold on right here and I'll bring you one. What are you drinking? I'll get us a round," she said.

OK so I thought this whole experiment thing was working well.

"I'll have an Amstel Light," I said.

We sat down and talked. She had a green martini, but I wasn't about to ask her to try a sip just yet. She'd brought a copy of her CD, and I payed her for it. Fifteen dollars. Miyuki was fit, real firm, jet black hair, blue lipstick which was a nice touch and I liked the shape of her eyes.

"So how did you find out about my show?"

"I was outside my friend's condo, taking a walk, when I saw your poster on a bulletin board."

"Wait a minute- was it at the Avalon Condominiums by any chance?"

"Yes. Why?"

"That's where *I* live!"

"Get out! No way. I live only five minutes away. I must tell you; full disclosure, I've never even been to this club or even this town. I love it so far but it's a first for me out here," I explained.

"I'm not surprised. Forest Loop is the sticks, but I'm a regular here and people come from all around sometimes. And of course, we have a steady stream of locals too. Hey wait right here. I have to use the ladies' room, okay?"

Jane would get a kick out of this. Unbelievable. Maybe they even know each other. I should text her. I pulled out my phone and sent Jane a text that said I took her advice in the experiment with reaching out to someone and getting out of my comfort zone, and it worked really well. I didn't say *who* I reached out to or give any details just yet though.

Miyuki returned to our table, and a man walked by congratulating her on the show, placing his hand on her shoulder. "Thanks Harvey," Miyuki responded.

"Excuse me Miyuki, sorry about that," I said while my cell phone notified me of another text. It was Jane and her response was: 'That's great Jake but follow through and do it again. Take another risk right away if you can', she wrote me. I thought for a second but didn't want to lose my flow with Miyuki, and after all, *right away* meant *right away*.

"Miyuki, how about we get together sometime? We live so close to each other."

"I'd like that. What do you have in mind?" she asked.

"You look so fit; you must jog. Right?" I said.

"Yeah. Do you know my father had a dream for me to be in the Olympics? Yes, it's true. He said anything is possible in America, and my parents were really driving me towards that sort of thing. They're from Japan originally, and you know, although I didn't make it that far athletically, at least on a professional level, I don't regret how anything has turned out in my life. I can genuinely say that I am living my dream."

"So, would you like to take a jog tomorrow morning? I've been really working on getting back into shape and thought it couldn't hurt to ask you."

"Sure. Come by 9 a.m. My place is number 101."

I drove home along the quiet roads leading me back to my apartment. From the rural landscape of Forest Loop to more familiar suburbia. I definitely had an amazing night and escaped reality for a few hours. Kind of like my dream. But this could only be the beginning.

9

I drove to Miyuki's condo, number 101. I had to drive past Jane's condo just to get there which was awkward. I hope she didn't see me, but then again, maybe it would get her attention. I'd have to tell her sooner or later. I think I *want* Jane to know. Could it make her jealous? When it comes to Rick or any other guy she's dated, I can't say it's about jealousy. It's just life and the way things happen.

Miyuki and I made our way outside after she gave me a quick tour of her residence. It was immaculate and enticing. Although there were many pictures of her on the wall with so many people that it was overwhelming. I had the feeling she'd turn out as another friend rather than love partner.

"Should we take my car?" I asked.

"No, not this time, follow me." She was wearing Muay Thai shorts that showed off her muscular thighs. The kind used for kickboxing. Really short shorts that were obviously sexy on her. No blue lipstick this time. She put her hair back and tied it with a hair band.

We started off with a light warm up pace that felt comfortable. I read somewhere that it's running etiquette to keep the pace of the slowest person in the group. "You never knew about this trail?" she asked, sounding surprised.

"No."

"I guess your friend Jane never showed you it. That's OK; I'll show you. We'll get a really good workout. That's what you want right?"

"I want to really get a good sweat going. I'm ready to do it all day."

"Good, let's *do it*. Well you know what I mean."

As we jogged and jogged, we passed ponds and streams, leaped over logs, and avoided big rocks and mud. We heard birds singing, frogs croaking, and even chipmunks chirping. Coming to the end of the path, we were faced with a busy road that I recognized. There we waited for the cars to clear out. She held my hand and said. "OK let's go for it!"

It felt so good to have her touch me like that. However long this day lasted, I'd never forget it. The portion of the trail we just finished connected with another trail that I did find myself familiar with. I was experiencing a bit of a runner's high and I think she was also. Completely loosing track of time, it felt like we were jogging on the never-ending trail. I knew I'd burn a ton of calories today, which is a great thing.

Later, as we returned to her place, I downed two glasses of water. I was soaking with sweat and there's no way I'd continue our date like that. Once again, she wasn't shy at all, offering me the use of her shower. I did think ahead by bringing a change of clothes. I grabbed them out of my car. I made my way to the bathroom and stripped off all my clothes while looking in the full-length mirror. Hey, I'm making progress, I thought to myself, noticing the definition in my muscles gradually coming through day by day. As I went to slide open the shower door, her black bra and panties fell to the floor landing on my feet. I don't know if she left them there on purpose, but it made me feel excited. Not knowing where to put them as I held them there in my hands against my bare body, I placed her intimates on the bathroom valet. I took a refreshing warm shower. The flow of water from the shower head was strong and invigorating. I tried out her cherry blossom shampoo and used a bar of turquoise colored soap. I got dressed and splashed on some Aspen cologne I had with me in a travel sized bottle. Once again, nostalgia from when I was a teenager in the late 90s. I couldn't really fix my hair since I didn't remember to bring any styling products, but I'd gotten a haircut two weeks ago and it was shorter than usual so it looked good just in that messy tousled kind of way. I wore my contact lenses today as opposed to my glasses because jogging is easier that way.

"You look good!" She said while rubbing her hand on my head, further messing up my hair. "And I like the outfit- very preppy."

I had khakis and a green checkered shirt on. "Follow me," she said. She sat down at the couch and I was in the armchair.

"You know... I don't bite; you can come sit over by me."

Once again, I heard that line about coming

closer and a person not biting, and I almost had to laugh at it. I moved over closer to her and we talked.

"I really love your CD. Your music reminds me of Basia. You know, the jazz singer," I said.

"Of course. I love her work. I met her in New York City once."

"Really, you did? That's cool. Well, I just think you're incredible," I told Miyuki. I really didn't know what more to say. I felt at a loss for words. Literally the words wouldn't come out of my mouth. I was like paralyzed in a way. Not physically but on some level, I was just frozen. It's another side of me. I thought about how talkative I am with Jane but how quiet I was at that moment with Miyuki.

10

It was time again for my next therapy session at Jane's. Same time. Same Place. Sitting across the room from her on the comfortable armchair. Sinking into the cushion. Letting my sore muscles relax.

"Can I get you anything? Water? Coffee?" Jane asked.

There was something in her voice I recognized as different. She was uptight. Upset about something. This was not the Jane I knew. Jane was much different than this. Jane was ordinarily, well, perfect and today she wasn't. Standoffish and I could tell by her body language as well.

"Yes, coffee please."

When she came back, I looked at her and said, "What's wrong Jane?"

"Nothing. What are you talking about?"

"You're not yourself."

"I saw your car here the other day. What were you doing here?" she asked.

"Do you remember your suggestion for me about breaking out and talking to someone? The *experiment*?"

"Sure. Did you meet someone new?"

"There's this jazz club." I cleared my throat. "Miyuki plays the piano and sings there."

"Her...oh yes..." Jane breathed in deeply. "She plasters her ad on the bulletin board, taking up all that room. Personally, I've not listened much to her music, but I hear she might be fairly good, *I guess*."

"I'd love to tell you about the jazz club and all, but I don't know if you really want to hear about it," I said.

"Sure, you can if you *want* to, but I think we should continue off from where we were last session."

"OK well you asked me about Sandra, that girl from the hotel that I was dating and what happened there. I didn't get around to all the details in our last session but after her and I went our separate ways.... well about a year to the day she walked into the hotel lobby after midnight as I was covering the graveyard shift. Just like that, out of the blue. I wasn't even in contact with her at that time."

"I'm interested. Continue."

"Well, I was taken by surprise. Not seeing her or hearing from her in a year's time," I said.

"I bet."

"So, we reconnected for a few minutes and Sandra said she was working down the road, etc. Then a couple nights later she calls me up while I was at the video store, browsing through the action and thriller movies, trying to decide. I miss those days, by the way, when there were video stores, that is. And so, we're on the phone, she invites me over, suggests we watch the video together. So, I go. It's late in the evening. I bring a bottle of wine. She and I drink through it and we finish the movie then head to bed. But I was kind of drunk. Acting totally normal and stuff but I just wonder if I didn't finish off that bottle with her, would I have been more ready to take things further. I know what you're thinking: contrary to conventional thinking. Usually you get drunk and want to fool around, but in my case, not this night. I didn't feel comfortable taking it to the next level. We're there on her bed, under the covers. The lights are out, and after a couple minutes she leans over and whispers in my ear, 'Do you want to have sex?' and of course I was taken aback. Part of me liked it and the other part of me was just not comfortable."

"So why not and what did you tell her?"

"I explained to her that I wasn't comfortable with it and blah blah blah, but in reality, I just didn't feel like taking off my clothes. I should have told her that, but I didn't."

"Maybe if you just told her directly the reason you didn't want to have sex was because you didn't feel comfortable naked, she would have convinced you otherwise. And you know you were in great shape at that time Jake," Jane said.

"I know. Here I am wishing I were in shape the way I once was, yet back then I still wasn't satisfied with myself. Truth be told, I'm getting back into shape the way I was and then some."

"That's good Jake. Although you look great the way you are."

"I had another revelation. You know sometimes I get down about things like we all do, and then I thought about how I would feel if everyone was on my side. Rooting me on. It's not realistic, I realize that, but just stay with me here. Put yourself in this position. What if everyone loved you and wanted to see you do well and was cheering you on in life? It made me realize that I care too much about what other people think. In reality it's never going to be that way where everyone is going to be rooting me on in life and wanting to see me do well, so there's got to be another solution which is obviously not caring so much about what other people think of me."

"Easier said than done, right?" Jane responded.

"How about breaking it down to individual topics. What if a guy is losing his hair, and he just can't accept it? What if everyone out there loved the way he looked? Would he be unhappy about his hair anymore? Strange, I know, because it's never going to work out like that but what if he became happy with his new look? Took a 'bald is beautiful' approach. It goes to show you we have more control over our lives than we think. The power of the mind. If we just learn to be happy with ourselves."

"What about me? Not everyone can have a body like Miss Miyuki jazz extraordinaire," Jane replied.

"Jane, I *lust* your body. I mean I *love* your body." I can't believe I said it, but I did. There's no taking it back. A tingling sensation ran through me.

She got up. "Look at these thighs! And look at my arms. I don't have a body like *hers*. You are talking about not wanting to take off your clothes with Sandra ten years ago when you were in impressive shape and you think *I* look great. Well Jake, you've got awfully high standards for yourself."

"I was rejected so many times in my life that I have to live up to some standard in order to feel good about myself, and it's not easy to get to that standard when something goes wrong. I get off track. But I'm going to do it and I'm going to get in touch with who I used to be and I'm going to become the real Jake again. To be the best I can be. Mind, body, spirit."

I didn't know that Jane was so hard on herself also. Sure, Miyuki does have a rock-solid body, and I liked her looks, but I was more attracted to Jane. I couldn't believe anything would last with Miyuki anyways. Our session ended. I walked out to my car and drove home.

11

The hotel was surprisingly slow all week. Glancing at the computer, I saw the occupancy and knew that day to day it would rise and fall because people would cancel, and some would just not show up, giving us no notification of their change in plans. In the end it would go up as reservations were made online, over the phone and in person. Still it's a nice relief to have it slower. I don't want the aggravation, regardless of our potential revenue.

I signed into Facebook from my desk in the back-office area and scrolled through the screen. Hmmm... I saw a series of photos. Jane and Rick. Rick and Jane. Hugging. Laughing. Smiling. Kissing. Oh goodness. I can't take this. Raul walked by and looked at my screen. "That's him, right? Rick. With Jane," Raul asked.

"Yes."

"Let me look closer. He's got beautiful eyes."

"Thanks Raul. You sure know how to make me feel good."

"But I saw you were at some kind of jazz club last Friday? You checked in online. What was that all about?"

"Yeah. Not just that Raul. Not just that..I had drinks with a woman named Miyuki and we're seeing each other."

"Look at you. You stud. Have you been working out more? You've lost weight. You keep going and you'll be back to your old self again Jake."

"Thanks Buddy."

"I'm impressed you're seeing the jazz singer."

"She's really amazing. Her music and everything. I'm just surprised you knew who she was. Even I never heard of her before I saw her ad on a bulletin board."

"Yeah, she was on the local news. They did a segment on her," Raul mentioned as he strolled over to his desk.

I was relieved to get out of work and put

Miyuki's CD in my car right away. I stopped at the coffee house around the corner to get a dark roast for the ride home. Pouring in the milk, I stirred it around and even sprinkled some cinnamon and nutmeg on top. I was feeling pretty good about myself, dating her. Like a self-esteem booster. I dialed Miyuki from inside the coffee shop before leaving.

"It's not you Jake. It's just we don't have that connection I'm looking for. I need that connection. You're a great guy. You're going to find someone else. I just know it," Miyuki explained.

"So it's over? OK that's alright, I understand. I'm disappointed but..." I began to tell her while I felt a powerful current of emotions coming up to the surface. I was going to burst into tears but held down the emotion.

I think the pressure of everything just hit me all at once. Work. Jane. Miyuki. I got in my car and drove home listening to her CD while a tear rolled down my cheek. Something that hasn't happened to me since, well, since I can remember. I was sad. But I was OK with being sad because under the surface I knew things were going to be alright. Something about that dream still stayed with me. It'll always stay with me. That lake. That coffee house with my friends. Well, dream-world friends anyways. The pool tables. Them trying to fix me up with Misty. Who was Misty? And what did she look like...I wonder. Where was that lake? It felt like another state. Another world. Another reality.

12

At least another day of work at the hotel is over. I'm home to relax and decompress. I still have my coffee in hand since I drink it slowly. If I were more like most people, I'd take Miyuki's CD and smash it. But me being me, I'll probably pick it up every once in a while, and play it, daydreaming about my short-lived relationship with her. I sit down on my couch and put on the crime mystery network. Another true crime show is in progress, and I lean back into the couch wondering how things came to this. Jane and I love to watch these shows. It's what we have in common. She also tells me I can be a psychologist without the degree because of all the insight and knowledge I have. That's nice of her, but I want more than just nice. The temptation is driving me crazy. Although most of the time I block her out of my mind as far as romantic opportunities go since she's unavailable, yet she did seem jealous of my relationship with the jazz singer. I bet she'll be happy it's over now. If I can't have Miyuki and I won't attempt to try with Jane, then I'll have to find someone else. There're millions of available women on the planet, so no big deal, right?

I was starving. But I wanted something healthy. Not just healthy, *super healthy* to keep me on track. I hopped in the car and went down to the health food store. I picked up a bowl of a South American quinoa black bean soup with collard greens. It was also cooked in lime and orange juice, plus cilantro. Talk about flavor. This should be good. Also, a serving of spicy tofu, lightly fried and topped with crushed peanuts, cilantro, basil, and a slice of lime. So what if the health food store was next to Jane's office. I wasn't going there to see her, but to eat a healthy meal. Just my luck, there she was when I walked out. I saw her taking a break, getting some fresh air. I waved from a distance, then walked over to a bench where she sat.

"It's over Jane. Between Miyuki and me. Just like that. And I'm sad."

"Come on up to my office, you can eat there if you like. I was just going to have a smoothie myself." It's actually my first time here at her office since we always have our sessions at her condo. We climbed the stairs up to the third level, and she gave me a tour.

"Nice office."

"Yeah, I can't complain."

"Well, I suppose being here, we don't have to worry about Rick walking in," I said.

"Oh Jake. Wipe that smirk off your face."

I tried some of my soup and a bite of my bread. "No, it's just that I don't feel comfortable around him," I said while chewing. I know I hit a nerve with her by bringing it up.

"You're jealous of my relationship with him. Is that it?"

"You're jealous of my relationship with the jazz singer?" I answered her question with a question.

"What relationship?" Jane responded.

"Touché."

"Oh, shoot, I forgot I have someone coming in for a session now. I'll have to ask you to leave. I'm sorry, but can you finish your food at home?" she said.

"Sure, that's fine."

I walked out and took the elevator down. Stepping outside, I juggled the rest of the food while forgetting to take the bag I had it in. I pushed the front entrance door open and dropped my box of tofu on the stoop. Luckily, it didn't pop open. A lady there picked it up and handed it to me. *Who's this?* I thought.

"Thank you," I said.

"Anything good?" she asked.

"Spicy tofu. I've come to realize I can enjoy any kind of tofu."

"I've never had tofu," she said.

"What can I say about tofu? It's a food without taste to begin with, but it takes on the flavor of whatever you're cooking it with. Kind of a like a sponge. And really just some salt and pepper fried in oil is enough to make it taste great. Would you like to try some? It's still warm," I said.

"Sure, why not," she said.

I stabbed a cube of tofu with a plastic fork and placed it in her mouth. Waiting with anticipation, I stood there. She slowly chewed, looking happy.

"That's really good. Thank you," she said.

"What's your name?" We both said it at the same time, then laughed.

"OK, you first," she said.

"I'm Jake."

"I'm Juliette. Friends and family have tried to call me Julie, but I like Juliette better."

"OK Juliette. Would you be interested in maybe having tofu together sometime? Or a coffee?" I asked.

"I'd like to very much."

"How about tonight?"

"Tonight," she said smiling.

"Yes."

"I'm going to an appointment here and I should be ready by say, seven," she said.

"Meet me at the coffee house on the corner of Tenth and Lake? You know that place Uncle Javas?"

"Sure, yeah, I know it."

"OK, see you then."

13

This was amazing. Talk about a turnaround. I met Juliette at Uncle Javas and she was wearing a conservative outfit, a business suit. It looked good on her. She was thin, but it wasn't that I preferred thin, yet it was her chiseled, strong features and the uniqueness of her face that appealed to me. Her distinct voice, I found sexy.

We ordered our drinks and she had a lavender flavored hot latte which I'd never tried before myself.

"Here, have a sip," she handed it over to me."

"Mmmm that's really good."

I think I was in love with Juliette already. I sipped my coffee, stirring the metal spoon around in the ceramic cup even though it was already mixed. I didn't use sugar, but I did have extra milk as usual.

Juliette explained to me that she never gained weight if she had something sweet, whereas I told her that it was a major struggle on and off for me to lose weight and that I really did enjoy my coffee unsweetened the way I did. An acquired taste. I told her it took me forever to finish my coffee because I savored it. I appreciated the bitterness of it.

"You can give me some of your weight and we can call it even. I'm too skinny," Juliette said.

I smiled, not knowing how to respond to what she said. I knew I was on the right path and looking better each day as far as my weight loss went. When I recently saw my weight drop to a new recent low on the scale the other day, I felt more in control of my life. I love the way she looks but it wouldn't make one difference to me if she gained weight either. The Jake mentality for attraction to women is this: variety is the spice of life-beautiful women come in all different shapes and sizes. I just liked her and wanted to be with her so far. I found our chemistry was good although we hardly knew each other. I felt more of a natural urge to want to be with her romantically as the minutes passed.

When I asked her to come back to my place for a drink, she did and once we got on the couch, I put music on the television. We continued to make conversation. The music was a new age station, the melodies were soft and gentle, combining the sounds of pouring rain and thunder plus other elements of nature with instruments. I got our drinks from the kitchen. Two bottled beers. We took a sip or two and placed them down on either side of us. Nervously drinking from our bottles every now and then. The sexual tension was so thick you could cut it with a knife. We turned to each other and made eye contact. I leaned forward and kissed her, and she pushed her lips forward into mine. It was like a super charged magnet. I felt passionately excited and impulsive as my heart raced. It was all happening so fast. I was horny. I wanted her so bad and she was showing me she wanted me too. Our tongues were intertwined, dancing together in our mouths. I held her bottom lip between my lips pressing gently then sticking my tongue back in her mouth, running my hands through her lengthy light brown curly hair. She undid the clip and her endless luxurious hair flowed out. I felt her hair in my hands, exploring the texture. She ran her fingers through my hair also. She kissed me on my forehead. Slowly and gently she traveled down, kissing me on my cheek, neck and on my chest.

I took off my shirt. She took off her shirt, revealing her dark red bra. She undid her bra and her small perky breasts popped out, pointing towards me. I was incredibly attracted to her, like no one else in the world. I felt her body, running my hands down her shoulder going over her chest and slowly down her ribcage and stomach. Juliette leaned her back into the couch and I kissed her body all over. When I was kissing her tight stomach and making my way down, my lips touched her belt. She took off her belt and pulled down her pants. I kneeled on the carpet and looked between her legs, admiring her. I gently rested my head on her soft cotton panties, feeling the fabric on my face.

"I want you so bad Jake," Juliette said in a sexy low voice.

I massaged her long sexy thighs. she had firm lean legs like a marathon runner. She was a dream come true. Her fair creamy colored skin was warm to the touch. I massaged her quadriceps, inner thighs and hamstrings first slowly and gently and then more firm and deeper while she moaned. "That feels so good," she said.

I held her hand and we got up. Pausing for a moment, neither one of us knew what to say. Instead of going to the bedroom, we talked about how so quickly we felt right together and wanted to make things as close to perfect as we could. We even talked about one day maybe getting married and sleeping together on our honeymoon for the first time.

"I want to see you again as soon as I can Jake."

"How about you come over tomorrow morning at eight and I'll take us to breakfast at that famous bagel place. You know the one next to that red barn."

"Yes, great." She and I embraced each other, and she squeezed me so hard, but It felt so good. I held her firmly in a hug and we didn't want to let each other go. Then I kissed her on the lips, and we wished each other a good night.

"Drive safe dear!" I said. Thinking about our conversation at the coffee house earlier, I marveled at how sweet and kind she was. The kind of woman I dreamed of having in my life.

The following day

Juliette arrived a little early and while I was getting out of the shower, I saw her standing by my desk. "What are these notes here?" she asked, leafing through my journal.

"Oh, that's my dream journal. You know, interpretation and stuff."

"I hope you don't mind me. Am I being nosey?"

"No, that's Okay," I responded.

I had mixed feelings about it. I didn't feel mad at her for looking through my stuff. I was concerned, maybe cautious on the one hand but on the other hand I wanted her to be interested in all details about me. I can't really say any of my ex-girlfriends were the jealous type. I always figured though that if I had a jealous girlfriend, it would be a sign that she really cared and wanted me all to herself. She really loves you and is obsessed with you a bit, is that a bad thing? I know it could turn out to be, but it'd be nice to have that kind of affection.

I never discussed Jane with Juliette. Or Juliette

with Jane for that matter. She never asked me why I was exiting the office building yesterday. There were plenty of other businesses in that building after all. It would come up sooner or later and I'm known as "honest Jake" so I can't lie to her. What would I have to lie about anyway?

We drove over to the bagel place, holding hands while in the car. When we got out, we walked over to the red barn next door and we looked at the horses for a moment. She reached for my hand, squeezing it for a second, and we walked in to order our breakfast. Customers looked over at us, admiring how much affection we had for each other. I held her hand, and we pressed up against each other. Her hair had an orange honey blossom scent that I savored. A gentle current flowed through me while I was attached to her.

14

Two weeks later...

It was odd. I didn't have anything set up with Miss Jane PHD, but what would I tell her? I was passionately making out with one of her clients- almost ending up in bed. Oh my God, she'd be shocked! First Miyuki, although nothing happened between her and I, but still Jane didn't take it so well. Sure, it was more of a passive aggressive response to my relationship with the jazz vixen but how would she like Juliette and I together? Why should I care? She's with Rick after all. Maybe I should make her jealous and post some pictures on social media with the new love of my life. Hmmm.

I had one week off from work beginning today, and to celebrate, I rounded up a couple friends. Matthew, my old buddy from college, and I asked Raul to come along since he was off work from the hotel by now. The three of us headed to the sports bar, which was a fun spot almost any night of the week.

As soon as we walked in, I saw Samantha. She was Jane's best friend, however, I never got along with her. Or was it she who never got along with me? Basically, I saw her as a bitch, and I just felt she saw me as someone beneath her socially. It felt like high school all over again with Samantha.

"Gentlemen," I said, speaking to my friends. "You know Samantha, right? She's across the bar over there. A wise man once said, 'When you say to the universe 'gimmie, gimmie, gimmie' the universe responds, 'gimmie, gimmie, gimmie,' but when you buy your enemy a round of drinks...well then, good karma."

They both looked at me puzzled and I responded, "OK, I changed the quotation around to suit my needs, but you'll see."

"Hey Samantha, how's it going?"

"Hi Jake. Hi Raul, Matthew."

"Can I buy you a round?"

"Ummm sure."

"This round is on me guys, all of your drinks. Let's do a shot of say, Jägermeister?"

"OK sounds good."

"Yeah good with me. Thanks!"

"Sure."

"Thanks Jake."

And we chased down our ice-cold shots with the drinks we had in our hands. I bought Samantha a cosmopolitan. I was on vacation. Why not. You attract more bee's with honey, like they say.

"Jake, you're not so bad you know."

"I'm *good*," I responded.

"I don't mean it like that. I mean sometimes in the past you've been such a quiet guy that I guess I was kind of, well, I suppose I passed judgment on you without really knowing you all that well. I'm seeing another side of you now and I kind of like it."

"Thanks. Have you talked to Jane lately?" I asked.

"Sure yeah. I'm going to be honest with you.

When she got back with Rick, she asked for my advice constantly. And I told her that Rick was an Adonis and a gorgeous hunk and all that stuff, but she wanted you."

"Really. Tell me more."

"Rick's cheated on her before and she doesn't really trust him."

"I see."

"*I* want Rick at this point, and she can hand him over to me," she said taking a sip of her cosmo. "But I now see that I was wrong about you. You're just different. But Jane, she's different too. Maybe you guys have more in common than I realized. I would tell her things, like to think carefully about who she chooses to be with, and how if you *really* wanted her Jake, you would have manned up and just made the move with her by now after all these years."

"Okay I see your point," I said.

My phone notification went off and I picked it up to see who the text was from. It was Juliette saying she loved me and was looking forward to our date tomorrow. That made me happy. I stopped for a second and took a breath. Next, another text came through with a picture of a green rose with a black background. It had water droplets on it. Underneath the rose was an explanation from Juliette: You are like this green rose, classy and mysterious and beautiful to me. Your whole aura is a work of art. I felt moments like these were the kind you remember all your life. I was delighted and felt complete with her in my life. I waited all these years and had failed relationships. Maybe this one would be right in the end.

"Who was that," Samantha asked.

"Oh, just someone I'm seeing, Juliette."

"Wait, Juliette, the one who is going to therapy with Jane?"

"You know about that?"

"This is getting interesting," Raul interjected.

"I second that," Matthew added.

"It's the alcohol talking now. Oh shit." She sighed and put her drink on the counter then picked it back up and guzzled the rest. "Can you buy me another? Make it a beer this time."

"Sure, bartender, she'll have a pint of the..."

"Make it an IPA, thanks."

"And thanks Jake," she took a swig of the beer and set it down. We all looked over at her, hanging on her every word.

"Okay listen, Jane and I were talking over drinks. Surprise, surprise. We got pretty sloshed and she told me stuff."

"Like about me probably."

"No, not you."

"Sure, I believe you."

"Anyways, we're getting off topic here. She said this Juliette woman is like super ugly...emaciated..." Samantha took a sip of her beer.

Now the three of them looked at me. I furrowed my brows and didn't know what to say.

As our night came to an end, we ordered a taxi to take us back to our own abodes. As I returned to my living room couch, I kicked up my legs on the ottoman and felt contented. I was still buzzed from the alcohol, to add to that I felt happy to be in love with Juliette. I was shocked at what Samantha said about her. I knew she was unique, but beauty is in the eye of the beholder. I had to laugh about the fact that Jane still didn't know about my relationship with her. Well that is unless Juliette told her in one of her recent therapy sessions. Well, let's face it, Samantha, her best friend would tell her everything anyways. But Samantha didn't know how passionate I was about Juliette. I only mentioned I was seeing her.

I got a call out of the blue from Jane. "Jane! It's been so long."

"Yeah, I felt bad. And now I feel kind of blue," she said with a glum tone of voice. We both paused for a moment.

"Well it's official. Rick's out of the picture and he's even threatening to sleep with my best friend Samantha. I know, I know, you think she's a bitch. She's rough around the edges is all," Jane said.

"Are you drinking?" I asked her.

"Why?"

"I am."

"Okay I am too. You got me."

"I can take a taxi over if you'd like. It's only five minutes," I suggested to Jane.

"Sure. I'd like that," she said.

The taxi dropped me off and Jane greeted me with a hug at her door. I liked the hug and it was a nice touch since I don't remember ever hugging her before. Isn't that weird? I thought.

"Come sit down."

"OK."

"Would you like a lemon lime margarita? I've

got them mixed up in the kitchen. On the rocks okay?"

"Sure, that would be great."

"We sat down far across the room from each other like we would in a therapy session."

"I want to put on my psychologist hat now Jake. Is that Ok?"

"Yeah. There're probably things I could discuss and get off my chest. I mean, we didn't really end on a good note last time," I said.

"No, we didn't." She took a couple sips of her drink and set it down by the lamp on the coaster. "I'd like to do a little experiment-like a word association exercise."

"That sounds really interesting. OK."

"When I say *lake*, what comes to your mind? Don't think long and hard about it. Just go with your instincts."

"Um ok how about clear, clean, fresh, pure, rejuvenating."

"OK good."

"What's next?" I asked while she and I sipped on our margaritas.

"*Coffee house.*"

"I think warm, inviting, intellectual, comforting, also... invigorating, energizing."

"You're doing good," she said.

"*Pool table.*"

"I think concentration. Peace of mind. Focus. Fun," I responded.

"*Misty.*" Jane said.

"This is kind of weird Jane. You're reading my mind or something. It's like you know about this dream I had."

"What dream? Tell me about your dream Jake."

"I had this dream and all these things were in it that you mentioned. It was the most relaxing and peaceful dream I'd ever had. There was a lake in the distance, and I was in this coffee house with some friends and Misty was discussed but I'd never seen her. My friends in the dream tried to fix me up with her. There was a pool table also, it was really more of a hang-out spot. Like something you see on a TV show. It was all really kind of mysterious. Now that I think of it, it's probably got something to do with the teenage years I missed out on in life. Although we were all adults in the dream. You know, like our current age. I was looking forward to meeting Misty, but I woke up and that was it."

"You've never seen this woman Misty? She's not a real person?"

"No, but I thought it would come to be in life. Maybe it has. You know, somebody to symbolize Misty. First there was Miyuki after the dream. And she did play in this mysterious little town I'd never been to, you know, where the jazz club was. We know things didn't work out with her and then there was umm....uhh.."

"What? Who?" Jane asked.

"You know. You know things you're not telling me," I said while she gulped down more of her citrus cocktail and looked away.

"You're seeing Juliette," Jane responded.

"I am. That's right," I said.

"She's incredibly self-conscious Jake, fragile even. Don't lead her on. She'd be lucky to find anyone. You don't belong with her. A good-looking guy like you."

"Lead her on?" I asked.

"What could you possibly see in her? You're not actually romantic with her, are you?"

"I find her very attractive and we're intimate but we're not..well this is really personal."

"No way, I don't believe it," Jane said.

"Yes. I think she's gorgeous. By the way can I have another one of these?" I held up my empty glass.

"Sure OK."

We both got up and walked to the kitchen. As we did, we walked close to each other. Our clothes even touching, and I could smell her perfume. "That's nice perfume," I said.

"Thank you. I'm mad at you."

She fixed us up more drinks in the kitchen while I stood up, leaning my hand on the kitchen table.

"You and her together, I just can't picture it. I don't want to!"

"And you slept with Rick."

"Of course, I slept with Rick!" she exclaimed while stirring our cocktails.

I walked over to her and took the glass out of her hand, thanking her. We sat at the kitchen table, only about a foot apart from each other, making eye contact as we spoke.

"As your therapist and as your friend, I want

you to know that your dream was revealing to me and I've made some interpretations about it. You might not like everything I'm going to say. This Misty woman from you dream- you're searching for her and she's not real. You're looking for someone. Anyone to make you feel happy. Your desperate for love. So desperate in fact that you'll fall in love with someone without even caring who they are or how they look."

"That's not true. I care about people's morals. I care about making a connection. I care about being with someone who is good and who feels right for me," I explained.

"How about the jazz singer? Was she right for you?"

"She was a dream come true that ended before it really got started."

"Ok so you really didn't get far with her?"

"I got nowhere sexually with her, but she did leave her black bra and panties on top of the shower door. What a tease or it could have just left them there by accident. She's too busy anyways. I knew it wouldn't last with her," I explained.

"Oh, poor Jake. Those bra and panties are probably engraved in your mind!"

We stopped for a while and just sat there. Without knowing what to say or do next, we enjoyed our beverages. She put her hand on my thigh. "That felt good," I told her.

"You know Rick is gone for good. He's out of my life. I don't want him. I never even really loved him," Jane explained.

"Maybe that's the alcohol talking?" I asked.

"No, I don't know what it was with him, but he's not the only man who's been in my life. And you Jake, you've had your dry spells but remember back when you were just eighteen years old?" she asked.

"Yeah. That's back around the time we met."

"You were like Prince Charming. I wanted you so bad. There I said it," Jane waited for my response.

"I always thought you were cute Jane, but at that time I didn't think of pursuing you as a girlfriend. Maybe it was my subconscious mind telling me you and I were not a romantic possibility. The door to that world was shut. You were a girl who was a casual friend that I sat next to in class. And the bunch of us sat and talked at lunch sometimes.

I guess deep down what I'm saying is, I thought I wasn't good enough for you."

"I know, you don't have to explain any further. I'm your therapist. I know you in ways maybe you don't even know yourself." She put her hand back on my thigh and then ran it up towards my hand and left it there.

"Let me give you a massage Jane."

Her eyebrows raised and after a second, she told me she'd like that.

We moved over to the couch and Jane shut the blinds and lit up two large candles. She brought me a small bottle of massage oil, scented Jasmine. She put on some music, then sat on the couch turning her back towards me, then leaning into me. I put my hands on her shoulders and she took a deep breath. "That feels so good Jake."

I rubbed her neck and ran my fingers through her hair. I caressed her ears and gently touched her checks and forehead. I applied a firmer pressure and kneaded her upper back. She sighed. After about ten minutes, without asking me about it, she took off her shirt. I didn't say anything, but my heart beat a little faster. I pressed my fingers into her soft skin and felt the heat of her body. Applying more oil, I rolled my knuckles down the middle of her back and towards her jeans. I massaged her lower back region, getting closer to her jeans. "That feels incredible."

"I feel good doing it also. It's like an energy," I responded.

I massaged as low as I could go without putting my hands down her pants. I could see her panties were a pastel yellow color. I was turned on so strongly but wanted her to tell me what she wanted. Without saying anything she reached her hands behind her back and untied her bra strap. I took a deep breath and placed my hands where there was a mark left by her bra strap across her back. Massaging that area gently, then pressing my thumbs into her muscles in a circular motion. She leaned back into my chest, resting her head. I could smell her shampoo and her perfume. I looked down at her soft breasts and her stomach. I held her bicep in my hand and rubbed it then traveled all the way down to her forearm and hand. I massaged her palm and fingers, then the other arm starting at the shoulder working my way down. Again, all the way to the fingers, massaging each individual finger. She lied down on the couch and I massaged her feet, sliding my finger between each toe. When I finished, she sat up on the couch as did I. Her bare chest exposed. I looked at her and admired her beauty. She leaned forward slowly.

"No, stop. Jane, we can't do this."

"It's only a kiss," she said.

"But I'm in love with Juliette. I've only given you a massage and I can live with that." She put her shirt back on without the bra. We got up, and I knew that I had made the right choice, morally at least. "We can sleep together in bed, but only sleep. We can't do anymore. Is that OK? I would drive home but I don't have my car and after all these drinks maybe it would be easier to just get some sleep," I said.

"No, you should go. I'm calling you a cab Jake."

"I don't want things to be over between us Jane. Whatever it is we have, it's something."

"But you don't want me like that."

"I want you but I'm with Juliette."

"Just like I wanted you, but I was with Rick," she said.

"So, this is goodbye for now," I said.

"But not forever," she responded.

When my cab arrived, and I was on my way

out, I reached in to give her a hug. We embraced each other firmly and I felt her soft chest pressing up against me.

"Oh wait. I probably should give you back those DVD's you lent me."

"No that's OK. You hold onto them. Maybe someday....we can discuss them...I don't know."

I waked outside through her front door. When would I be back? I didn't know. I didn't live far away after all. I never really knew how strong she felt about me all those years? Who would have thought? But lately, life has been full of surprises. Maybe I'd always have a connection to Jane for the rest of my life.

Adam Kovynia was born in 1981 in Connecticut, as a first generation American. He grew up attending public schools in Southington and later graduated from Paier College of Art in Hamden, Connecticut where he majored in illustration. He has also taken courses at Rochester Institute of Technology (RIT) in New York state. Adam has worked in the hotel business as a night auditor and in a variety of retail jobs selling everything from eyeglasses, clothing, luggage, coffee, music and movies. He enjoys vegetarian cooking, weightlifting and jogging. He loves coffee, music and movies from the 80s and 90s, reading books especially in the genre of personal memoir, spirituality, self-help, and true crime. "Healing Balm Hidden Desire" is his third book. He is single and will continue writing and selling books and artwork. He would like to get involved with public speaking and also traveling to states in the Midwest.